JR. CHAPTER BOOK

THE
BAILEY SCHOOL
KIDS

P9-ELV-179

JR. CHAPTER BOOK

THE BAILEY SCHOOL KIDS®

REINDEER DO WEAR STRIPED UNDERWEAR

by Marcia Thornton Jones and Debbie Dadey
Illustrated by Joëlle Dreidemy

SCHOLASTIC INC.
New York   Toronto   London   Auckland   Sydney
Mexico City   New Delhi   Hong Kong   Buenos Aires

To Lydia and Logan, may all your
holiday wishes come true!—M.J.

For Alex and Becky Dadey and McKenzie Gunderson—
who do NOT wear striped underwear,
but are very magical creatures.—D.D.

To Nathan, Noa, and Marin whose names are at the top
of Santa's VERY NICE LIST! — J.D.

ISBN-10: 0-439-87630-3
ISBN-13: 978-0-439-87630-8

40 39   1 7/0

Printed in the U.S.A.
First printing, November 2006

CONTENTS

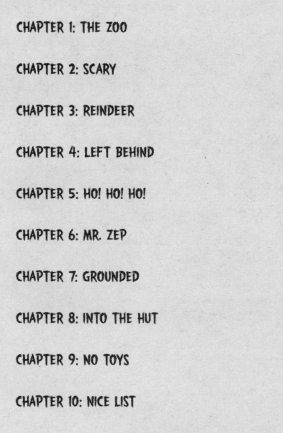

1

THE ZOO

"This is the best day ever!" Eddie yelled as he raced off the bus. It was the week before Christmas. His class was taking a field trip to the Bailey City Zoo.

His best friends Howie, Melody, and Liza climbed down the steps behind him. Liza pulled her hood up over her blonde hair. Melody put on green gloves. Howie zipped up his coat.

"Smell that fresh zoo air," Eddie said with a laugh.

WILD BOAR

Liza held her nose. She liked animals, but she did not like stinky smells.

Melody patted Liza's back. "It's okay," Melody told her friend. "It's not too stinky."

Pee-eww!

"Come on, Liza," laughed Eddie. "You'll get used to the smell once we get going!"

"We need to wait for our teacher," Liza said.

Eddie didn't like to wait. He wanted to run all over the zoo. His teacher had other ideas.

Mr. Zep held his hand out.
"Stop!" he warned.

2

SCARY

Eddie skidded to a stop.

"This zoo has wild animals that could eat second-graders in one bite," Mr. Zep told his class. "Stay with your partner. I don't want anyone getting lost."

In her mind, Liza saw herself getting lost. First, she was in a dark cave with bats chasing her.

Next, she was in a pool of water with a shark chasing her. Then, she was in outer space with aliens chasing her.

"Let's stay together," Liza told her friends. "I'm afraid of getting lost."

"Let's go have fun," Eddie said. "Being scared is silly."

"No, it isn't," Liza told him. "Everyone is scared of something."

"Not me," Eddie bragged. "I'm the bravest kid in the world." He grinned and rubbed

his hands together. "Lizards and snakes. Tigers and bears. Claws and fangs. I can't wait to see them all."

Then Eddie jumped in front of Liza and roared.

"AAAAAHHHHHHH!" screamed Liza.

3

REINDEER

Howie grabbed Eddie's cap and bopped him on his red hair. "Be nice," Howie told Eddie. "Liza's right. It's okay to be scared."

Liza looked ready to cry. "Eddie makes the animals sound like monsters," she said.

"Don't worry," Melody said, patting her friend on the arm. "The only monster here is Eddie."

Eddie roared like a monster again.

"There are lots of nice animals to see," Howie added. "We'll start with those."

Melody and Howie led Liza down the path.

Eddie flapped his arms like wings when they passed the buzzards.

He growled when they passed the bears.

He used his arms to make giant alligator jaws when they passed the alligators.

"Don't they have nice animals like bunny rabbits in zoos?" Liza asked.

Eddie hopped like a bunny and pretended to eat Liza's ponytail. "I am a giant rabbit and I'm going to eat you up," he said.

BOING

"Look," Melody said, pushing Eddie away from Liza. "These should be fun to see." She pointed to a sign that said REINDEER.

Eddie groaned. "Reindeer are boring. If I wanted boring, I would have stayed at school," he said. "I want fun."

"That isn't boring," Howie said.

He was pointing at a pen, filled with Christmas trees. A little hut sat nearby.

An animal looked at the kids. On its head were giant antlers. The animal had big brown eyes and a giant black nose. It was a reindeer, alright. It was a reindeer wearing long underwear with big red stripes!

4

LEFT BEHIND

Melody rubbed her eyes. "Can that be real?"

I don't believe it!

Could it be?

"It looks real," Howie said.

"That's the silliest thing I've ever seen," Eddie yelled. "An animal wearing underwear is crazy!"

Liza smiled. "I think it's cute," she said. "Besides, they're not underwear. They're pajamas."

"They look like underwear to me," Eddie said.

The reindeer looked at the four kids. Then it sneezed.

The reindeer took a deep breath and put its nose to the ground.

Snowflakes fell gently on the reindeer's back.

"He looks sad," Liza said.

"Reindeer don't get sad," Eddie said. "I bet his antlers are too heavy."

"Why is a reindeer in the zoo?" Melody asked. "Shouldn't it be at the North Pole getting ready?"

"Ready for what?" Howie asked.

"Christmas!" Melody said. "Everyone knows that reindeer help Santa, just like the elves."

"There must be a reason why this reindeer was left in the zoo," Liza said. "Being left behind would scare me."

"Everything scares you," Eddie told her.

Just then the door to the little hut swung open.

Howie blinked his eyes.
Liza gasped.
Melody gulped.
Eddie's mouth fell open.
"Is that who I think it is?"
Eddie asked.

5

HO! HO! HO!

Liza held her breath as a
man came out of the hut. He
wore a red suit and black boots.
He had a white beard and
bright blue eyes. His nose
was as red as a cherry.

"He looks just like the picture in my storybook," Melody said.

"I can't believe it's really Santa," Liza whispered.

Eddie shook his head. "That can't be him. Why would he be at the zoo? He lives at the North Pole."

"Eddie's right," Melody said.

"I am?" Eddie asked. He was not used to being right.

Melody nodded. "This is the week before Christmas. Santa has to be busy, busy, busy or we won't get everything on our lists."

The kids jumped behind a tree to watch. Santa went inside the pen. He carried a blue bottle over to the reindeer. "Ho! Ho! Ho!" he said. "This

33

medicine will make you feel like getting out of your pajamas."

He tipped the bottle into the reindeer's mouth.

"I think you are both wrong," Liza said. "That is Santa Claus. He is here to take care of his sick reindeer."

Howie nodded. "It DOES look like Santa. And he is giving that deer medicine."

"If you're right, then this is my chance!" Eddie snapped.

"I can ask him

for more gifts."

Eddie ran out from behind the tree.

"Wait!" Melody said.

WAIT!

Eddie was not good at waiting. He raced right toward the reindeer pen.

6

MR. ZEP

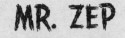

Eddie jumped on the fence and climbed.

Melody, Liza, and Howie ran after him, but someone beat them to Eddie. It was someone tall. Someone large. Someone mad.

It was their teacher, Mr. Zep.

He lifted Eddie off the fence. "Help!" said Eddie.

Mr. Zep shook his head. "Remember what I told you. There are wild animals in this zoo that could eat second-graders in one bite."

"But I have to tell Santa which presents to bring me," Eddie said.

Mr. Zep frowned. He looked to the right. He looked to the left. He looked at the monkey cage. He looked at the zebra pen. He looked at the reindeer. There was no Santa Claus.

Eddie couldn't believe it. Santa was gone! "He was right here," Eddie said.

Mr. Zep frowned even more and shook his finger in front of Eddie's nose. "No climbing."

NO CLIMBING

Mr. Zep walked away and Eddie shook his head. "Where did Santa go?"

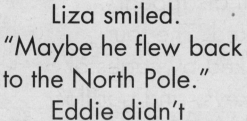

Liza smiled.
"Maybe he flew back
to the North Pole."
Eddie didn't
laugh, but he did look
at the reindeer. That's
when the reindeer
winked at him.

7

GROUNDED

"How does a man
in a red suit disappear?"
Melody asked. The four
friends walked by cages of
apes, monkeys, and gorillas.

"Santa Claus can do anything," Liza told her. "He's magic. That's how he can visit all our houses in one night."

Howie nodded. "It's true that Santa is magical," Howie said. "But I'm afraid he won't be visiting our houses this Christmas."

Eddie gasped.

Eddie moaned.

Then he grabbed Howie by the collar.

Tell me it's not true!

44

Howie patted Eddie on the back. "I'm sorry, Eddie. But I think Santa's reindeer has the flu. Soon, all his reindeer will be sick. Santa won't be able to deliver toys."

"What is Christmas without Santa and toys?" Eddie asked.

"Christmas isn't about getting toys," Liza said.

"It is for me," Eddie told her. "Anyway, I bet that's not the real Santa. I bet that's a fake reindeer, too. Not only that, I'll prove it to you!"

As usual, Eddie did not wait for his friends. He darted away.

Melody, Liza, and Howie followed Eddie. They sneaked by a group of second-graders.  They slipped by Mr.  Zep. They didn't stop until they reached the back of the reindeer pen.

"It can't be,"
Eddie said.

There wasn't just one reindeer in the pen.

There was a whole bunch of reindeer! There was even a reindeer with a really red nose. And they were all wearing their pajamas!

One reindeer sneezed.
Another one coughed. A third
one sniffed.

All of the reindeer looked
at Eddie.
"I told you this would
happen," Howie said. "Now
all of Santa's reindeer are sick.
There is no way they will be
able to fly on Christmas Eve."

I will save
CHRISTMAS!

"Not if I can help it,"
Eddie said.

"There is nothing you
can do," Melody told Eddie.

Liza patted Eddie on the
shoulder. "Melody is right," she
said. "It would take something
huge to save Christmas."

"Like what?" Eddie asked.

"It would take," Liza said,
"a Christmas miracle."

8
INTO THE HUT

Eddie pulled away from Liza. "I am not going to stand here and let Christmas be ruined," he told his friends. Then he ran to the front of the fence around the pen. He reached for the gate.

"You can't go in there," Liza said.

"It's against the rules," Melody added. "You'll get in trouble."

"I don't believe in rules," Eddie said. "And I don't care if I get in trouble."

"It could be dangerous," Howie said. "You might get hurt."

"No way," Eddie said. "I'm not afraid of anything." Then he pushed on the gate.

"No!" Liza screamed.

Eddie did not listen to his friend. The gate slowly swung open and Eddie ran toward the hut.

"We have to get Eddie out of there," Melody said.

Howie nodded. "Melody is right," he told Liza.

Liza sighed. She didn't want to go, but she was too afraid to stay by herself. They all went to stop Eddie, but he wouldn't stop. "I have to find out if that's really Santa," he said.

He reached the door to the hut. His friends were right behind him.

They knocked on the door. No one was there.

Eddie opened the door and stepped inside.

"Oh, no!" Eddie gasped. His knees shook. Eddie saw something that made him afraid. Very afraid.

9

NO TOYS

Two huge lists of names
hung inside the small hut.
"Nice List," Melody read
out loud.

"This must be Santa's list
of all the good kids," Liza said.
"Melody, do you see my name?
I hope it's there!"

"Of course your name is
there, Liza. I see my name, too!
And there's Howie's name."

Howie pointed to the
other list. "Naughty List,"
he whispered.

NICE LIST

Anna	Sam
Liza	Mark
Howie	Suzie
Jane	David
Martin	Melody
Clement	Matt
Howie	Vincent
Eric	Lucile

NAUGHTY LIST

Frank ✓	Eddie ✓
Susan ✓✓	Marsha ✓✓
Harold	Lyle ✓✓
Barry	Jillian
	Julian ✓

for Santa

MAGIC BOOK

TOYS

Eddie stood in front of the Naughty List. His name was on the list! A big red check marked his name. Many of the other names on the list had two red marks beside them.

NAUGHTY LIST

Frank ✓   Eddie ✓
Susan ✓✓   Marsha ✓✓
Harold   Lyle ✓✓
                      Lilian
                      Julian ✓

gulp

"Santa must be checking it twice," Liza said.

"Does this mean I won't get any new toys?" Eddie asked. He sat down on the floor. He didn't feel very good. He felt sick, just like the reindeer. What if his stocking was filled with lumps of coal?

What if his Christmas tree had nothing but coal under it?

What if his whole house was filled with coal for Christmas?

10

NICE LIST

"I've got to get off the Naughty List," Eddie said. He grabbed a pencil out of his backpack. Eddie started to mark out his name.

"Wait!" Liza said. "You can't do that! Something very bad will happen."

"What?" Eddie asked.

Liza shrugged. She wasn't sure, but she thought Eddie might get zapped by lightning. Or maybe a big wind would blow him away. A snow monster might even eat him. "Just don't do it!" she begged.

"I know how you can get off that list," Howie said.

"Tell me," Eddie begged. "I have to get off the Naughty List!"

"It's easy," Howie said. "Do something nice."

"Not that!" Eddie said.

Melody nodded. "It's the only way."

Liza patted Eddie on the back. "It's okay to be afraid. But you have to do it before Santa puts two checks by your name."

I will try.

Eddie took a big brave breath. "I will try," he said.

me?

"Come on, what animals should we see next?" Liza asked her friends.

"Why don't you pick?" Eddie told Liza.

Liza smiled and led them to the penguin exhibit. While his friends watched the penguins jump in and out of the water, Eddie sat on the floor. He took out his pencil and two pieces of paper. He wrote and wrote.

"What are you doing?" Melody asked.

"I made a get-well card for the reindeer," Eddie said, his face turning red.

"That was so nice," Liza said. "That will help them get well."

Melody nodded. "Reindeer are magical. I bet they know what you did."

"I made something for you, too," Eddie told Liza. He held up a paper.

Everyone was very quiet.
So quiet they all heard it at the
same time. It came from over
their heads. It was loud. It was
deep. It was happy.

"Ho! Ho! Ho! Merry
Christmas!"

Liza smiled. Melody
grinned. Howie laughed
out loud. Eddie almost fainted.

His name was no longer
on the Naughty List and he had
saved Christmas!